DACHSHUND DISCOVERIES: ON THE FARM

DACHSHUND DISCOVERIES

"On the Farm"

Breta Lee

BRETA LEE BOOKS
READ AND GROW

BRETA LEE BOOKS
(608) 317-0553
breta@copper-lily.com
www.bretaleebooks.com

This book is dedicated to my beautiful and talented daughters, Emma, and Eva. They have made me the proudest mom and inspire me to grow and reach my life goals. Thank you for your love and support. You are my greatest inspiration and sources of boundless pride.

Love,

Mom

There were two dachshunds named Cooper and Bear.
Bear - black and tan. Cooper - red hair.
They loved to run when the weather was good.
Discovering friends under dried stacked-up wood.

One day on the farm, so sunny and bright.
Cooper spotted an animal all
brown with some white.
It hopped quickly and quietly
into the bramble.
Can you guess what it was? Oh
please, take a gamble!

Bear joined Cooper tracking scents by the barn.
They scrambled and darted to avoid any harm.
Cooper barked loudly to alert Bear of danger.
They halted with verve, face-to-face with a stranger.

A four-legged friend with
red fur and a tail.
Jumped towards them while
snarling and let out a wail.
They sprinted and zigzagged
to the woods in plain sight.
Can you guess what it was?
You just might be right!

While sniffing around on the paths amongst trees,
The dachshunds uncovered some walnuts and seeds.
They pawed at them playfully and nosed them for a while.
Cooper gathered them together and placed seeds into piles.

A small furry friend with gray
fur and small paws.
Chattered loudly from branches
and scolded without pause.
The dachshunds looked up
to locate the sound.
Can you guess what it was?
There are many around!

Racing on trails made by new ATVs.
Bear and Cooper ran back to the farm with great ease.
They caught another scent going under a shed.
A deep and long tunnel was right up ahead.

A pudgy brown animal, standing upright and curious.
Made a dash for the hole which made Cooper so furious.
Chasing down underground and tunneling with great ease.
Can you guess what it was? Try your best, please, please, please!

Cooper picked up a scent by the reddish tin pole shed.
He darted by hay bales that were stacked up ahead.
Bear caught on quickly and joined with great eagerness.
Sniffing low to the ground with tremendous unevenness.

A black and white animal waddled up by a bale.
It walked very slowly, pausing to shake its grand tail.
The dachshunds saw movement from the corner of their eye.
Can you guess what it was? Can you give it a try?

Cooper and Bear saw the barn door was open.
They scooted through with ease even though it was broken.
Up the stairs to the right, they came to the hay mound.
They dove into the haystack and peeked all around.

A flapping of wings was
heard from above.
It flew through the rafters,
just like a dove.
Bear ducked down, but
Cooper was inquisitive.
Can you guess what it was? It
has camouflaged plumages.

The dachshunds dashed from the barn and down to the creek.
Exploring fields on the way, so green and sleek.
Their tails were wagging as they stopped by the water.
Cooper halted abruptly as his chest was much broader.

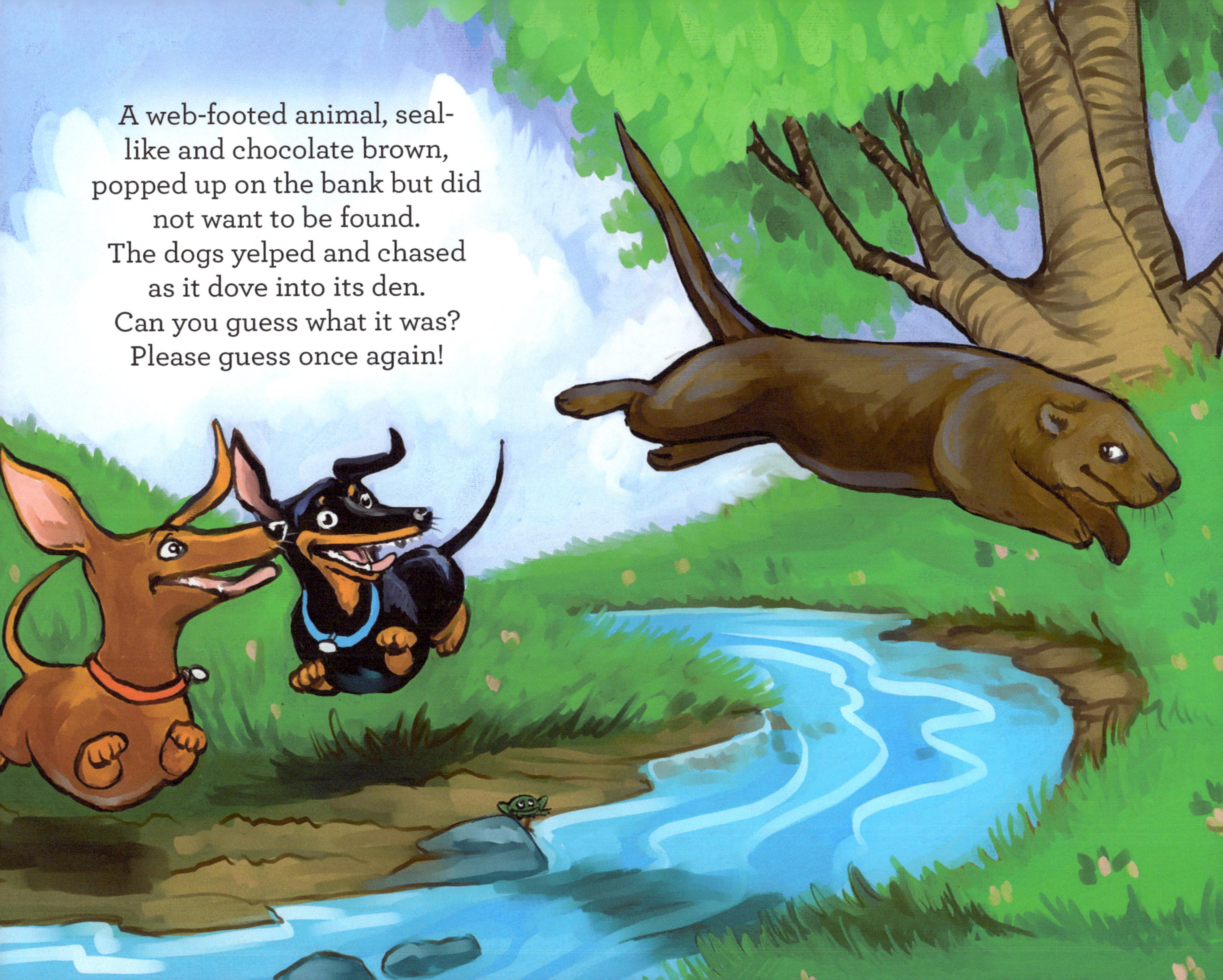

A web-footed animal, seal-
like and chocolate brown,
popped up on the bank but did
not want to be found.
The dogs yelped and chased
as it dove into its den.
Can you guess what it was?
Please guess once again!

Feeling tired from running, the dogs sat on the creek bank.
They laid down in the sun near a rusty cow tank.
Their ears were perked and tails wagging,
as they saw a brown animal whose branch it was dragging.

Sharp, long teeth and broad, flat, scaly tail,
An animal drug the branch to its lodge made full scale.
Bear and Cooper walked over to see the construction.
Can you guess what it was? It was quite a production!

The sun started setting as the dachshunds were walking.
They looked at one another as if they were talking.
The soft, gentle breeze made the evening so cool.
They trotted along the creek where they came to a deep pool.

Cooper spotted a tall creature with a rack and white tail.
It was taking a drink from the pool near the trail.
It looked up at the pups, gave a snort and a bleat.
Can you guess what it was? That would be sweet!

Their humans, Emma and Eva were calling their names.
"Cooper, Bear, Cooper Bear! Come home!" they exclaimed.
The sisters ran quickly down the driveway to greet them.
The pups lept in their arms, reunited once again.

The dachshund discoveries on the farm were so fun!
Cooper and Bear cannot wait to have more than just one.
Thank you for helping make predictions and guesses.
You named each animal, one of the most impressive successes!

FUN FACTS ABOUT DACHSHUNDS:

Size and Appearance

The Dachshund comes in one of two different sizes. There is a standard size, which can weigh between 16 to 30 pounds. There is a miniature size, which typically will weigh less than 16 pounds, often under 11 pounds.

Dachshunds have unique styles that their coats come in. One of the types of Dachshund coats is smooth and shiny, another is wiry and rough, and the third is a long-haired coat that is also smooth and silky. The classic colors are red/brown and black/tan. There are many other variants from those main colors.

Where Do They Come From?

As their name suggests, Dachshund originally came from Germany in the 1600s. They were bred for their unique shape because it helped them burrow into the ground to hunt for rodents and badgers. The word Dachshund is German for (Dachs)badger (hund)dog.

Additional Facts About Dachshunds

As pets, Dachshunds are friendly and easygoing, but they can also be very energetic and very brave. Because of their nature, they are very likely to chase smaller animals, like birds, rabbits, squirrels, and cats. They have also been known to dig up moles in the ground when they feel the vibration of the mole tunneling.

Personal Experiences with Dachshunds

Cooper

Bear

Cooper and Bear both like to tunnel under blankets to sleep. They enjoy spending time with their owner and family and will follow them everywhere. They even like to go for rides in a car or truck. Dachshunds are very smart and can learn tricks such as fetching and shaking or sitting up with a reward system. Potty training can take a bit longer than other breeds but once they learn it, they do well. We have a pet door that allows them to exit independently, which has been helpful.

It is important to take your dachshund to the vet to make sure their shots are up to date and to make sure their teeth are cleaned. As the dog ages, they may need to take a supplement such as glucosamine for their joint health. This helps if they have joint pain. Cooper is getting older, so I give him soft treats and soft dog food to accommodate him having teeth removed.

Dachshunds travel low to the ground, so it is important to check them for ticks. Dogs can easily get anaplasmosis which is a tick-borne disease, or full Lyme Disease. Always consult your veterinarian about your dog's health.

ABOUT THE AUTHOR

Breta Lee, a seasoned educator, Director of a Private School, Adult Day Services Program, Community Based Program, and CEO of CopperLily Digital Solutions LLC, a marketing agency in Wisconsin, brings her rich, 28-year teaching experience from both local and international classrooms to her writing. Her book, Dachshund Discoveries: On the Farm, is inspired by her life on the Lee family farm with her daughters and their dachshunds, Cooper and Bear. The farm, a hub for family gatherings and outdoor adventures, serves as the backdrop for her story. Today, she lives with her partner, Ben, on his family farm. Breta's passion for nature, conservation, and family is evident in her work. Through her book, she aims to foster a love for reading, nature, and the values of hard work and environmental stewardship in young readers.

Photo by Emma Lee

www.ingramcontent.com/pod-product-compliance
Lightning Source LLC
Chambersburg PA
CBHW041138100726
47911CB00005B/147